# The Joke Book

*By Catherine Hapka*

**HarperFestival®**
*A Division of HarperCollins Publishers*

# LITTLE GIGGLES

How did Stuart feel when George didn't
want to play with him?
**Mouserable.**

Why is baby Martha so good at basketball?
**She's an expert dribbler.**

Why did George start dreaming about
the sun?
**Because Stuart told him to "rise
and shine."**

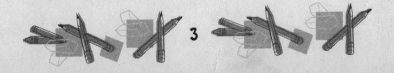

Why is Mrs. Little like a telephone?
**They both have rings.**

How did Stuart feel after being rescued
from the sink?
**He was completely drained.**

What is Stuart's favorite breakfast cereal?
**_Mice_ Krispies.**

**Mr. Little: Knock knock.**
Mrs. Little: Who's there?
**Mr. Little: Cash.**
Mrs. Little: Cash who?
**Mr. Little: No thanks, dear.
I prefer peanuts.**

5

Why did George take his soccer award for a ride on his bicycle?
**Because someone told him to put the pedal to the *medal*.**

What kind of umbrella does Stuart carry when it's raining?
**A wet one.**

Mr. Little: Why does Martha keep spitting out her oatmeal?
**Mrs. Little: She's just giving us some feedback.**

What two things can you not have for breakfast?
**Lunch and dinner.**

How many baby-sitters does it take to change a lightbulb?
**None. They don't make diapers that small.**

What has one foot and four legs?
**A bed.**

Will: Do Stuart and George like
playing soccer?
**Coach: Yes. They get a real kick
out of it.**

# BIRDBRAINS

**Margalo: Knock knock.**
Stuart: Who's there?
**Margalo: Beets.**
Stuart: Beets who?
**Margalo: Beets me!**

Margalo: Why did the pigeon cross the road?
**Stuart: It was the chicken's day off.**

What bird is with you at every meal?
**The swallow.**

What does Margalo do on Halloween?
**She goes trick-or-*tweeting*.**

**Margalo: Knock knock.**
Stuart: Who's there?
**Margalo: Boo.**
Stuart: Boo who?
**Margalo: Don't cry. It's just a joke!**

What do you call a bird with no eye?
**A brd.**

Why don't birds like to discuss their feathers?
**It's a ticklish subject.**

9

Stuart: Why shouldn't you grab Falcon by his tail?
**Margalo: It may be his tail, but it will be your end.**

What holiday is strictly observed by all birds?
**Feather's Day.**

Stuart: What steps would you take if Falcon were after you?
**Margalo: Fast ones!**

How can you tell that birds like shopping at sales?
**They're always saying "cheep-cheep."**

Stuart: Which side of a bird has the most colorful feathers?
**Margalo: The outside.**

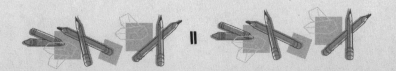

# PLANES, TRAINS, AND AUTOMOBILES

Why did Stuart do his homework in his plane?
**He wanted to pursue a higher education.**

Margalo: When is a car not a car?
**Stuart: When it turns into a garage.**

**Margalo: Knock knock.**

Stuart: Who's there?

**Margalo: Cargo.**

Stuart: Cargo who?

**Margalo: Cargo "beep beep!"**

What happened when Snowbell slept under the car?

**He got up *oily* the next morning.**

**Stuart: Knock knock.**

Margalo: Who's there?

**Stuart: Luke.**

Margalo: Luke who?

**Stuart: Luke out! Here comes Falcon!**

George: What ten-letter word starts with G-A-S?

**Stuart: Automobile.**

What happened when Stuart lost control of his plane?
**He got a crash course in landing.**

**Stuart: Knock knock.**
Margalo: Who's there?
**Stuart: Darren.**
Margalo: Darren who?
**Stuart: Darren young man in my flying machine.**

Where does landing come before takeoff?
**In the dictionary.**

**Stuart: Knock knock.**
Margalo: Who's there?
**Stuart: Lima bean.**
Margalo: Lima bean who?
**Stuart: Lima bean workin' on the railroad!**

# KITTY CAPERS

What is Snowbell's favorite TV show?
**The nightly *mews*.**

Why are cats such bad dancers?
**They have two left feet.**

How does Monty get rid of fleas?
**He starts from scratch.**

Snowbell: What kind of cat lives in the ocean?
**Monty: An octo*puss*.**

How can you tell the difference between a can of cat food and a can of dog food?
**Read the labels.**

**Snowbell: Knock knock.**
Monty: Who's there?
**Snowbell: Howl.**
Monty: Howl who?
**Snowbell: Howl you know unless you open the door?**

What happened to the cat who swallowed a ball of wool?
**She had mittens.**

What's Snowbell's favorite color?
**Purr-ple.**

Monty: How does a flea get where
he's going?
**Snowbell: *Itch*hiking.**

What kind of cats like to go bowling?
**Alley cats.**

Why did
Snowbell want
to visit a
bakery?
**So he could
loaf around
all day.**

What did the Martian say to the cat?
**Take me to your litter.**

George: Why does Snowbell snore
so much?
**Stuart: He's a *sound* sleeper.**

What's worse than raining cats and dogs?
**Hailing taxis.**

**Monty: Knock knock.**
Snowbell: Who's there?
**Monty: Butter.**
Snowbell: Butter who?
**Monty: Butter be careful when
Falcon's around!**

How can you keep Monty from smelling?
**Hold his nose.**

Why did Snowbell follow the chicken
across the road?
**Because he's a copycat.**

What's the difference between a cat
and a flea?
**A cat can have fleas, but a flea
can't have cats.**

Why didn't Snowbell believe he was getting
tuna for dinner?
**It sounded too fishy.**

Monty: What is a kitten after it's six
months old?
**Snowbell: Seven months old.**

What is Snowbell's favorite sport?
**Hairball.**

**Snowbell: Knock knock.**

Stuart: Who's there?

**Snowbell: Aesop.**

Stuart: Aesop who?

**Snowbell: Aesop I saw an angry Falcon!**

# FUNNY FRIENDS

**George: Knock knock.**
Will: Who's there?
**George: Don Juan.**
Will: Don Juan who?
**George: Don Juan to go to school today.**

Margalo: Did you hear the one about the garbage barge?
**Stuart: Yes. It's a load of rubbish!**

Will: Hey, George! Which hand do you write with?
**George: Neither. I usually use a pencil.**

Snowbell: My food tastes funny.
**Stuart: Then why aren't you laughing?**

**George: What has a bottom at the top?**
Will: I don't know. What?
**George: Your legs!**

Stuart: Did you hear the one about the pencil?
**Margalo: Yes, it was pointless.**

Will: What kind of table has no legs?
**George: A multiplication table.**

George: Why did the jewelry thief take a shower?
**Will: He wanted to make a clean getaway.**

Stuart: What do you call an overeducated plumber?
**Margalo: A *drain* surgeon.**

Will: Why did the cross-eyed teacher lose her job?
**George: Because she couldn't control her pupils.**

**George: Today, my teacher yelled at me for something I didn't do.**
Stuart: What was that?
**George: My homework!**

# FLYING HIGH

Stuart: Did you hear the joke about the broken egg?
**Margalo: Yes, it really cracked me up!**

What does a bird get when she's injured?
**_Tweetment._**

How do birds stop themselves in mid-flight?
**They use air brakes.**

Why do birds lay eggs?
**If they dropped them,
they'd break!**

Why do birds watch the news?
**To get the *feather* forecast.**

Margalo: Why did the chicken cross
the playground?
**Stuart: To get to the other slide.**

Why do birds fly south for the winter?
**Because it's too far to walk.**

Some birds were flying south for the winter. There was a bird in front of two birds, a bird behind two birds, and a bird between two birds. How many birds were there in all?

**Three birds, flying single file.**

Margalo: What kind of bird is always out of breath?

**Stuart: A puffin!**

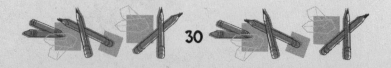

Where can Falcon always find diamonds?
**In a deck of cards.**

Falcon: Do you know your lines?
**Margalo: Nope. I'll just wing it.**

What kind of test does a bird take
in school?
**An egg-zam.**

What kind of birds are always unhappy?
**Bluebirds.**

How does Margalo stay so thin?
**She eats like a bird.**

**Falcon: Knock knock.**
Margalo: Who's there?
**Falcon: Alex.**
Margalo: Alex who?
**Falcon: Alex the questions here!**

Why did Margalo use hot rollers on her feathers?
**She heard that the curly bird gets the worm.**

Why do birds make good outfielders?
**They're good at catching flies.**

Falcon: Which weighs more, a pound of jewels or a pound of feathers?
**Margalo: Neither. They both weigh the same (one pound).**

What's the strongest kind of bird in the world?
**A crane.**

Stuart: What flies when it's on and floats when it's off?
**Margalo: A feather.**

Falcon had ten gold coins. All but seven got lost. How many did he have left?
**Seven.**

# NEW YORK SILLY

Stuart: What wears shoes but has no feet?
**George: The sidewalk.**

Mrs. Little: Did you hear about the smog?
**Mr. Little: You don't have to tell me. It's all over town.**

What do cars in New York have for breakfast?
**Traffic jam.**

What did one taxi muffler say to the other taxi muffler?
**"Boy, am I exhausted!"**

George: Why did the traffic light turn red?
**Stuart: You would too if you had to change in front of all those people!**

George: What building in New York has the most stories?
**Stuart: The library.**

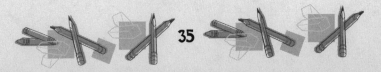

Who earns a living by driving his customers away?
**A taxi driver.**

Why is an elevator operator so happy?
**Because his job gives him a lift.**

Why are garbage collectors so unhappy?
**Because they spend so much time down in the dumps.**

Why was the street angry?
**Because it had been crossed so many times.**

Stuart: What's as big as a skyscraper but weighs nothing at all?
**Margalo: A skyscraper's shadow.**

Stuart: Where do birds invest their money?
**Margalo: The *stork* market.**

# A LITTLE MORE FUNNY STUFF

How does Mrs. Little feel when it's time to do the dishes?
**She gets that sinking feeling.**

Why did George stand on his head?
**Because his feet were tired.**

What did the principal say when Stuart and George were late for school?
**"Two Littles, too late!"**

What does Stuart put on his hot dogs?
**Mousetard.**

Who's bigger—baby Martha or her father?
**Baby Martha, because she's just a little Little.**

What do a baby and an old car have in common?
**They both have a rattle.**

Mr. Little: How do you make a milk shake?
**Mrs. Little: Jump out and yell, "Boo!"**

Was Stuart's trip down the drain scary?
**Yes, even the string was *a frayed*.**

Why was the plumber depressed?
**Because his career was going down the drain.**

**Stuart: What's the longest word there is?**
George: I don't know. What?
**Stuart: Smiles, because there's a mile between the first and last letter.**

Will: Why couldn't the elephant twins
go swimming?
**George: Because they only had
one pair of trunks between them.**

How did Mr. Little feel when he got a big
bill from the electric company?
**He was shocked.**

Why did Stuart bring his car to the soccer game?
**Because the coach told him to drive for the net.**

What's Stuart's favorite game?
**Hide-and-*squeak!***